THIS BLOOMSBURY BOOK

BELONGS TO

....

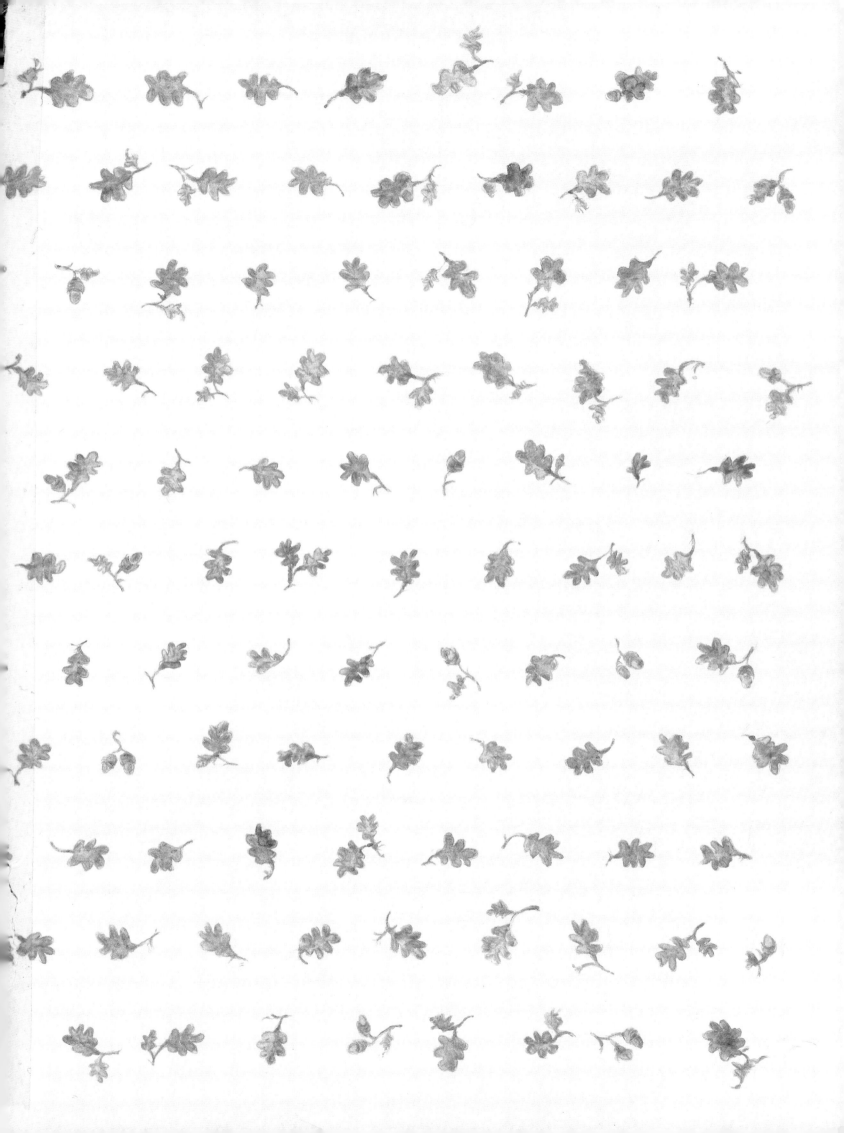

For Stephen and Liz Baird,
with many thanks – SG

For Paulina, Mary Elizabeth,
Dorothy and Valentina McNeill – ET

First published in Great Britain in 2002 by Bloomsbury Publishing Plc
38 Soho Square, London, W1D 3HB
This paperback edition first published in 2003

A CIP catalogue record of this book is available from the British Library

ISBN 0 7475 6112 5

Designed by Sarah Hodder

Printed in Belgium by Proost

10 9 8 7 6 5 4 3 2

No Trouble at All

Sally Grindley
and Eleanor Taylor

BLOOMSBURY
CHILDREN'S
BOOKS

Shhh! They're fast asleep.
Don't wake them up.

They're such good
little bears when
they come to stay.

I just have to say it's time
for bed, and off they trot
as good as gold.

When I was their age
I was full of mischief.

These old houses are full of strange
noises. I'd better just check those little
bears aren't frightened.

Not a sound.
I must have worn
them out.

I'll just fetch
my slippers.

Ah, here they are.

Their mother says those little bears can be very naughty. I'm sure that can't be true.

What was that?

I can't have closed the door
properly. Silly of me.

It's a beautiful night.
If it's sunny tomorrow
we'll all go for a picnic.

I'll pop and fetch
the picnic basket
from the shed.

Here we are. Tomorrow
I'll fill it with sandwiches
and cakes and chocolates
and drinks and off we'll go.

They deserve a treat,
those little bears. They're
absolutely no trouble.

No trouble at all.

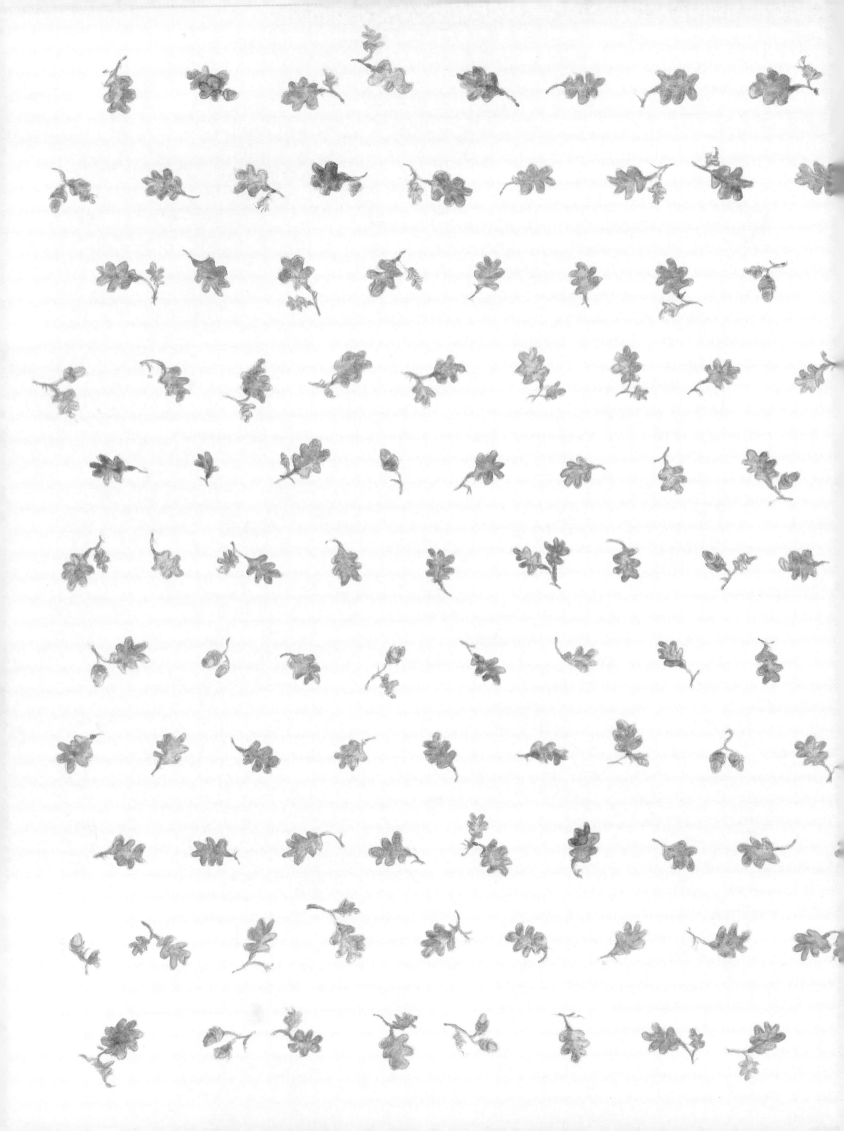

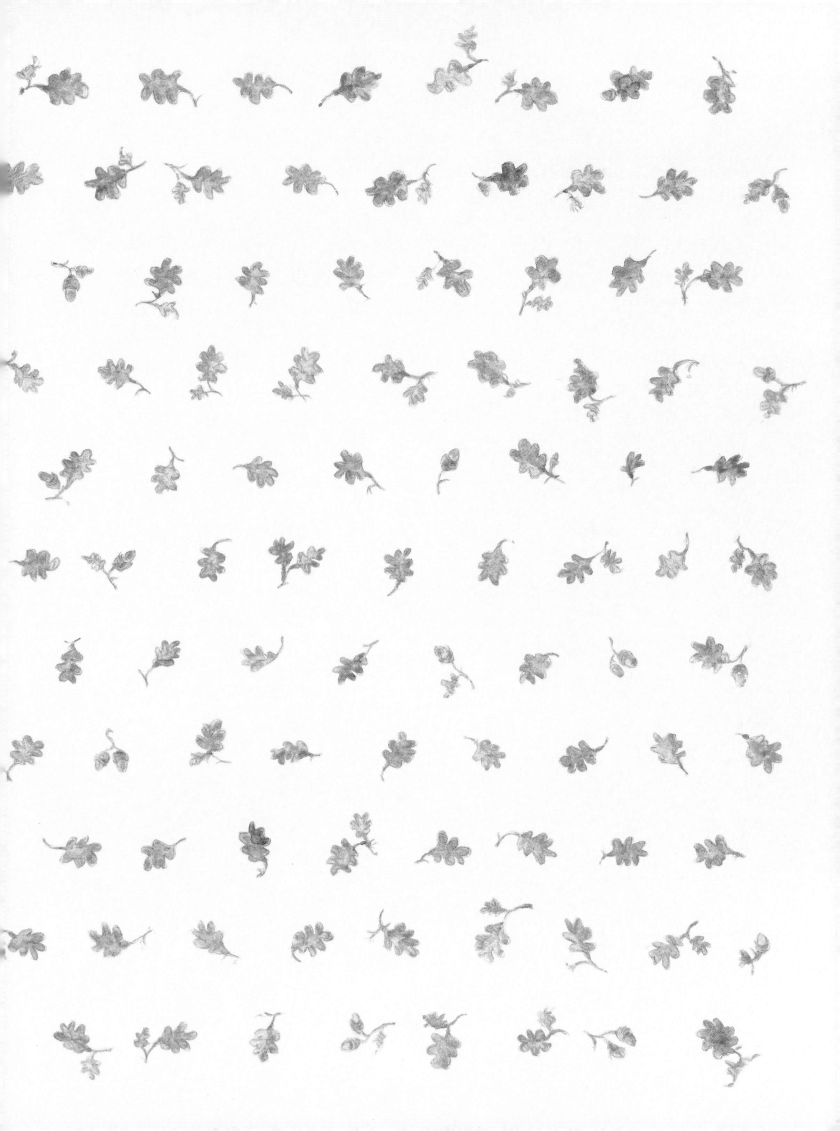

Acclaim for *No Trouble at All*

'The poker-faced text plays straight man to Taylor's charming artwork. Her illustrations of the impish cubs in a cozy tree dwelling make clear that the ursine siblings mean no harm' *Publisher's Weekly*

'A testament to unconditional grandparent love' *Kirkus Reviews*

Bad Hare Day
Miriam Moss & Lynne Chapman

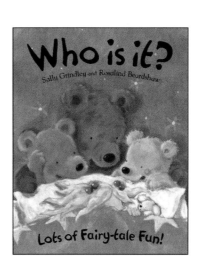

Who is It?
Sally Grindley & Rosalind Beardshaw

Run, Rabbit, Run
Christine Morton & Eleanor Taylor

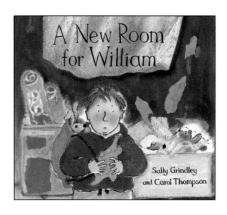

A New Room for William
Sally Grindley & Carol Thompson